OLIVIA™
Plays Soccer

adapted by Tina Gallo
based on the episode "Olivia and the Soccer Game"
written by Pat Resnick

illustrated by Jared Osterhold

Ready-to-Read

Simon Spotlight
New York   London   Toronto   Sydney   New Delhi

Based on the TV series OLIVIA™ as seen on Nickelodeon™

SIMON SPOTLIGHT
An imprint of Simon & Schuster Children's Publishing Division
1230 Avenue of the Americas, New York, New York 10020
OLIVIA Plays Soccer and *OLIVIA Goes to the Library* © 2013 Ian Falconer and Classic Media, LLC.
All rights reserved.
OLIVIA™ Ian Falconer Ink Unlimited, Inc. and © 2013 Ian Falconer and Classic Media, LLC
All rights reserved, including the right of reproduction in whole or in part in any form.
SIMON SPOTLIGHT, READY-TO-READ, and colophon are registered trademarks of Simon & Schuster, Inc.
For information about special discounts for bulk purchases, please contact Simon & Schuster Special Sales at
1-866-506-1949 or business@simonandschuster.com.
Manufactured in the United States of America 0713 LAK
This Simon Spotlight edition 2013
2 4 6 8 10 9 7 5 3 1
ISBN 978-1-4814-0019-0
These titles were originally published individually by Simon Spotlight.

Mrs. Hoggenmuller gathered
all the girls together.
"It is almost time for our
first soccer game," she said.
"Come get your uniforms!"

Olivia smiled and said,
"I will be wearing
the red shirt!"

But Mrs. Hoggenmuller said,
"The red shirt is for the
goalie.
I have selected Francine
to be our goalie."

The next day Olivia tried on
her soccer uniform.
"Green is not my color,"
she said.

"It looks fine," Mother said.
"Green is the team color."

Olivia was not happy.
She tugged at her shirt.
"It is too big," she said.

"When you are part of a team, you need to look like the rest of the team," Mother replied.

Olivia decided to make her own uniform.
She found a blue shirt and shorts, and red bows for her ears.

The next day was the game.
Olivia wore her own uniform.
But the other team was
wearing blue too!

"Olivia, you broke the rules," Mrs. Hoggenmuller said. "But since this is your first game, I will let you play."

Olivia took her place on the field.
But her teammates got confused and would not pass the ball to her.

Francine was not a very
good goalie.
The blue team scored ten
goals.
The green team lost.

The team blamed Francine
for the loss.
"It was not all her fault,"
Olivia said.

"Maybe it was your fault!"
Francine said.
"Everyone thought
you were on the other team!"

Olivia was surprised
by what Francine said.

Back at home
Olivia tried on her uniform
again.
"I think your uniform is cool,"
Ian said.

The next day Olivia went to
the soccer field.
"My mother says I do not
have to be the goalie,"
Francine said.

"I will do it!"
Olivia shouted.

Francine was so happy!
Olivia was such a good
friend to volunteer!

Olivia the goalie got to wear
the red shirt.
And Olivia was a great goalie!

The green team won!
"I knew I would play better
with the right shirt,"
Olivia said.

That night Father tucked
Olivia in bed.
"Good night, my little goalie."
"Good night," Olivia said.

Olivia hears the story
one more time before bed.

"'They lived happily ever
after,'" Mom reads.
"Good night, Olivia!"

"Come listen, and you can
check it out after.
'Once upon a time . . .'"

The storyteller is holding the book!

"I was about to read this for story time," he says.

"No, but I did find Julian," Olivia says, giggling.

"Is it there?" asks Ian.

"I think I see it!" yells Olivia.

"Ian, want to go on an
exciting adventure to look
for my book?" asks Olivia.
"That is not exciting,
but okay," says Ian.

"Dad, have you seen my book?" Olivia asks.
Dad has not seen it.
Olivia keeps looking.

"I left my book on a chair," says Olivia.
"Now it is missing."
"I will let you know if I see it," the librarian promises.

"Can I help you?"
asks the librarian.

Olivia looks for the book,
but she cannot find it.

"I will show you," says
Olivia. But the book is gone!

"That was almost as good as The Enchanted Pineapple Princess," Olivia tells him. "I do not know that one," he replies.

"'They lived happily ever after,'"
reads the storyteller at the end.

Olivia puts her book down
next to her.

"Can we listen to story time?" Olivia asks. "Sure," says Dad.

"Hold on to your book,"
Dad tells Olivia.
"Ian, can you drop the rest
into the slot?"

"But I am not done with mine," replies Olivia.
"We can renew it," says Dad.

"Ready to go to the library?"
asks Dad.
"Our books are due back
today."

"What are you reading,
Olivia?" asks Ian.
"The Enchanted Pineapple
Princess,"
Olivia answers.